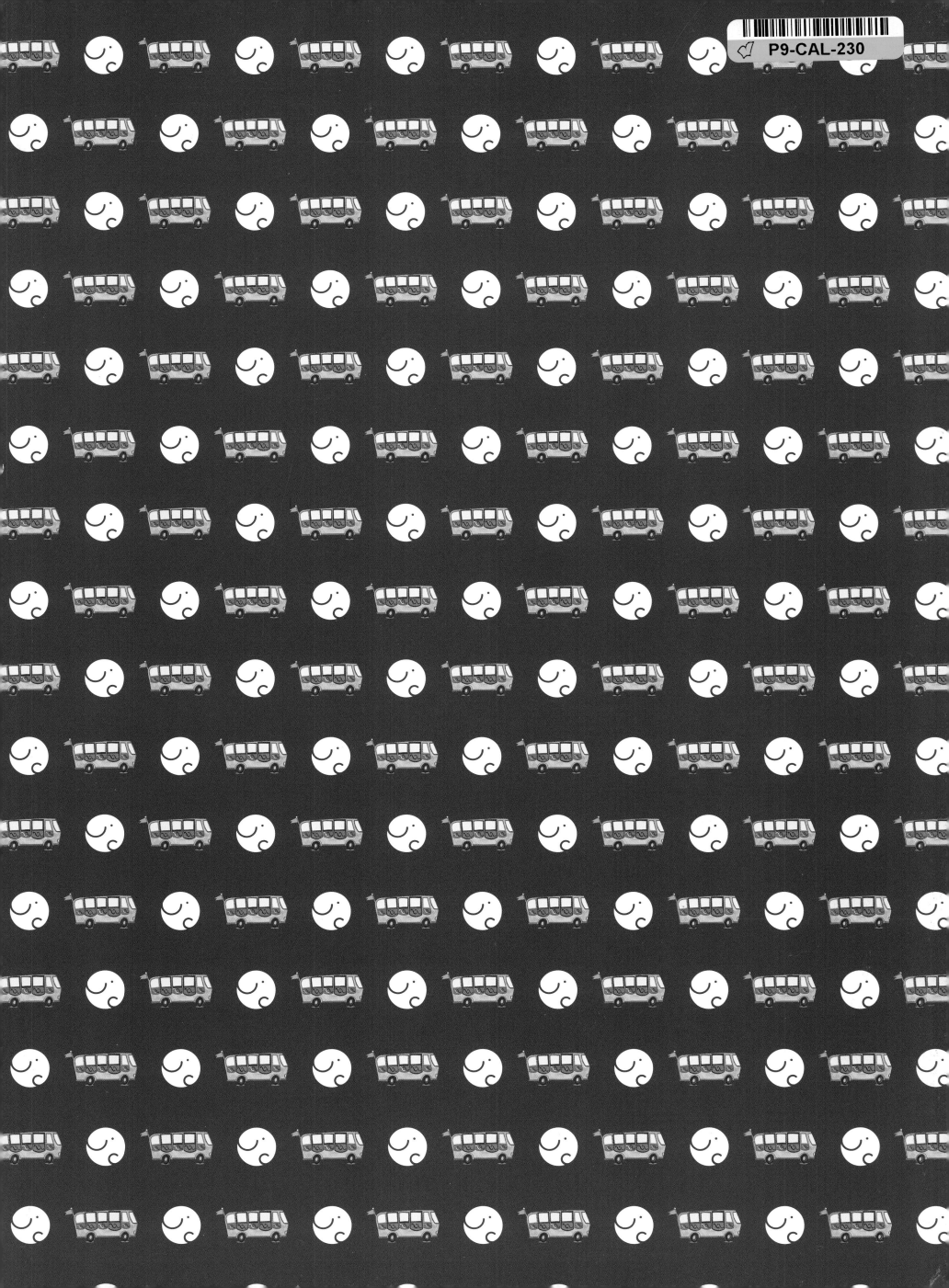

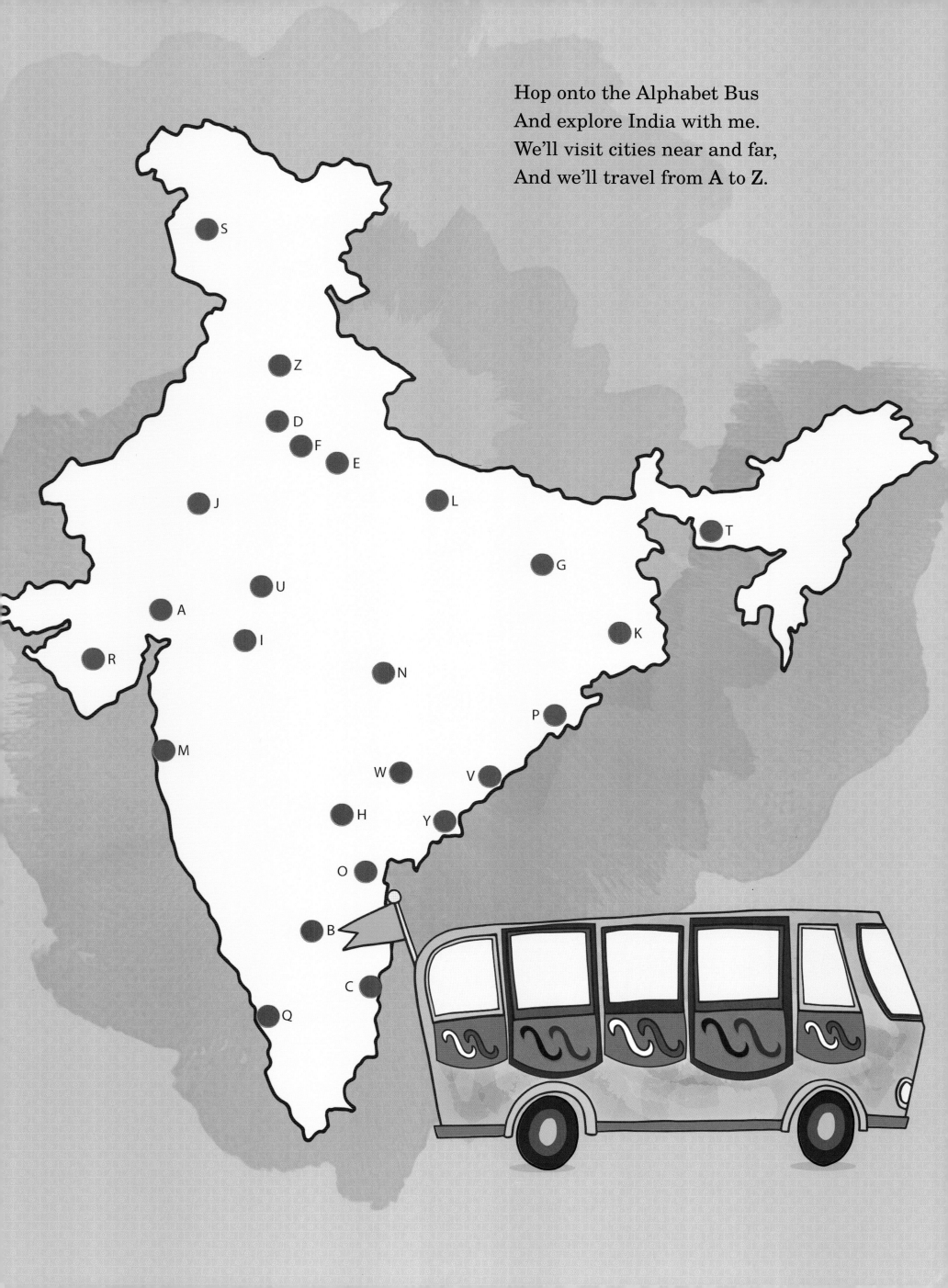

Hop onto the Alphabet Bus
And explore India with me.
We'll visit cities near and far,
And we'll travel from A to Z.

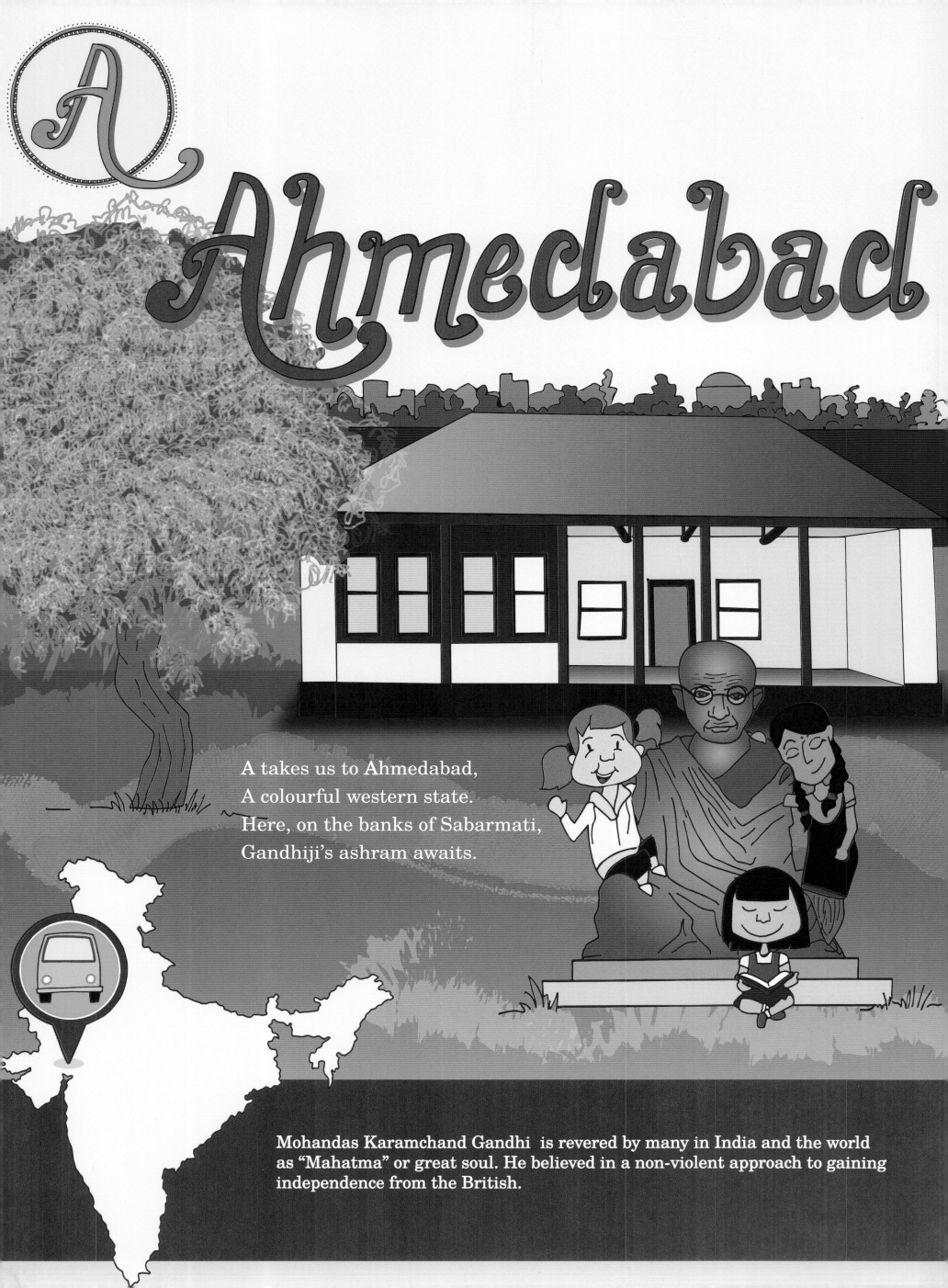

A Ahmedabad

A takes us to Ahmedabad,
A colourful western state.
Here, on the banks of Sabarmati,
Gandhiji's ashram awaits.

Mohandas Karamchand Gandhi is revered by many in India and the world as "Mahatma" or great soul. He believed in a non-violent approach to gaining independence from the British.

Bengaluru

B brings us to Bengaluru,
The sprawling city of high-tech.
The weather is good, inventions are too,
But traffic is so bottle-neck!

Bengaluru, once Bangalore, is called the Silicon Valley of India because of the many Internet Technology firms in the city.

C calls us to southern Chennai,
Where beaches are sandy and bright.
Dance and song fill festival halls,
And temple bells ring through the night.

Chennai

Chennai is the capital of Tamil Nadu. It was called Madras for a long time and Tamil is the local language spoken in the city.

NEW DELHI D

D for New Delhi, capital city,
Rich with history like the old Red Fort.
Here we can see the grand India Gate,
And Jama Masjid with its spacious court.

The Red Fort was built by Emperor Shah Jahan and it was the
residence of the Mughal emperors for about 200 years.

E is for Etawah in Uttar Pradesh,
Where we will next make our stop.
Near river banks of Chambal and Yamuna,
Cargo trains transport farmers' crops.

Etawah

Etawah is a city on the banks of the Yamuna River in the state of Uttar Pradesh. The city was home to many freedom fighters during the Revolt of 1857, also known as the Sepoy Mutiny.

F brings us to Faridabad
With its factories and crowded streets.
People work hard in this Haryana town,
And the town markets are full of sweet treats.

Faridabad

Faridabad is the largest city in Haryana. The Hindi language spoken here is an older form called Braj Bhasha which is quite different to hear.

G

GAYA

G is for Gaya, place of stories and myth,
With old buildings and narrow lanes.
We can visit where Gautama Buddha taught,
Or learn of great King Rama's reign.

Gaya is the second largest city in the state of Bihar after its capital, Patna,
and is a major tourist attraction.

Gaya is believed to be where the Buddha, then known as Siddhārtha Gautama, sat under the Bodhi tree and became enlightened. Gaya is also mentioned in the epic *Ramayana* as a place that Lord Rama visited.

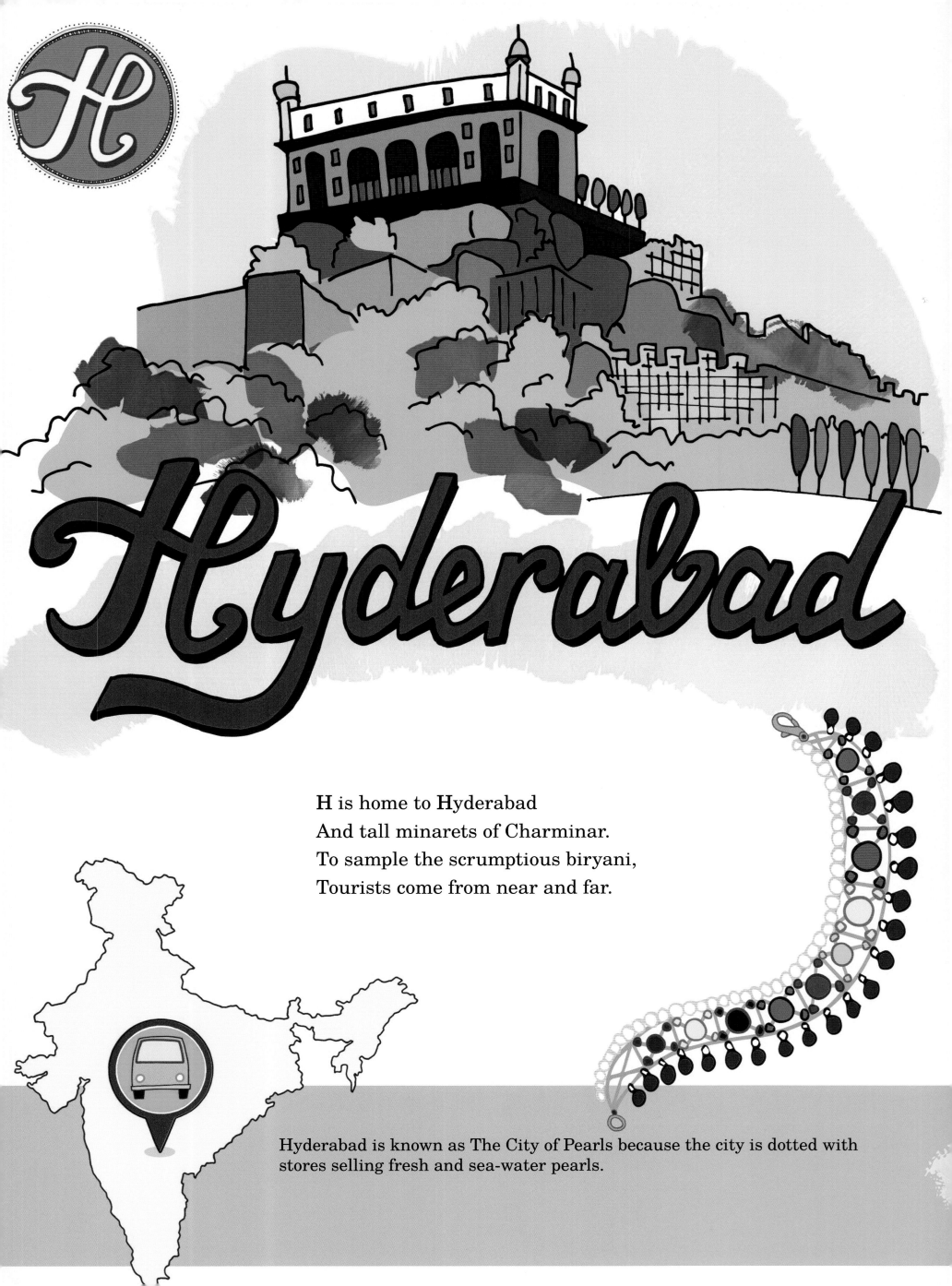

Hyderabad

H is home to Hyderabad
And tall minarets of Charminar.
To sample the scrumptious biryani,
Tourists come from near and far.

Hyderabad is known as The City of Pearls because the city is dotted with stores selling fresh and sea-water pearls.

I INDORE

I is for Indore in Madhya Pradesh.
Many languages are spoken in town.
The summers here are scorching hot,
Everyone has the same meltdown!

It can get to be 45 degrees Celsius in Indore on some summer days,
which is 113 degrees Fahrenheit!

Jaipur

J is for Jaipur, the famous pink city,
A dry desert where camels roam.
Study the stars at the Jantar Mantar
And gaze at the palace's dome.

The Maharajah of Jaipur believed that pink was the color of hospitality and painted the whole city that color to welcome Queen Victoria on her visit to the city in 1876.

K KOLKATA

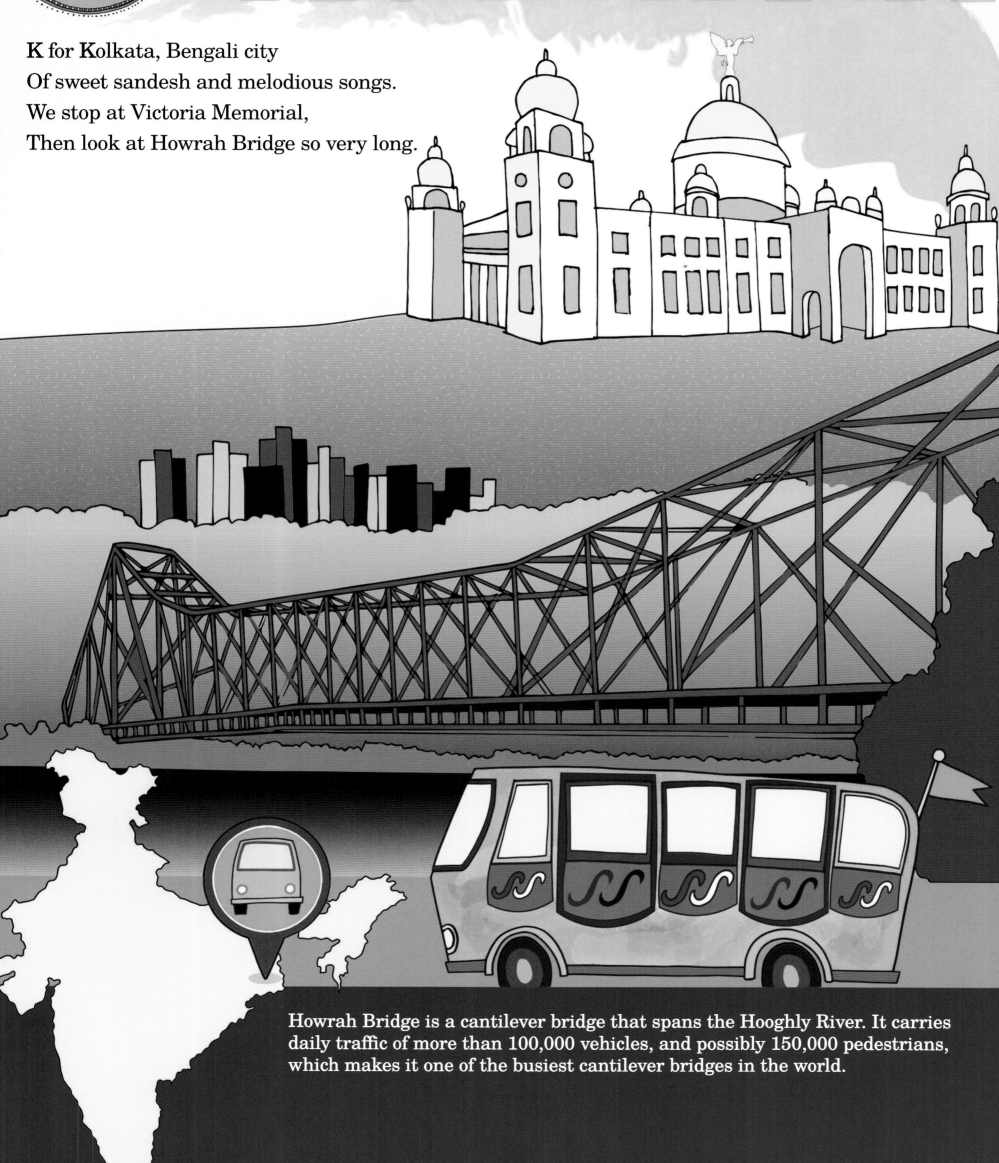

K for Kolkata, Bengali city
Of sweet sandesh and melodious songs.
We stop at Victoria Memorial,
Then look at Howrah Bridge so very long.

Howrah Bridge is a cantilever bridge that spans the Hooghly River. It carries daily traffic of more than 100,000 vehicles, and possibly 150,000 pedestrians, which makes it one of the busiest cantilever bridges in the world.

Lucknow

L is for Lucknow, a cultural city
With the grand Rumi Gate, sixty feet tall.
In this great place of poetry and music,
The noble Nawabs once ruled over all.

Many buildings and monuments in the city of Lucknow were influenced by Turkish architecture. The Rumi Darwaza, which is the historic gateway to the city of Lucknow, is similar to the Gateway to Constantinople. That is why the Rumi Darwaza is nicknamed the Turkish Gateway.

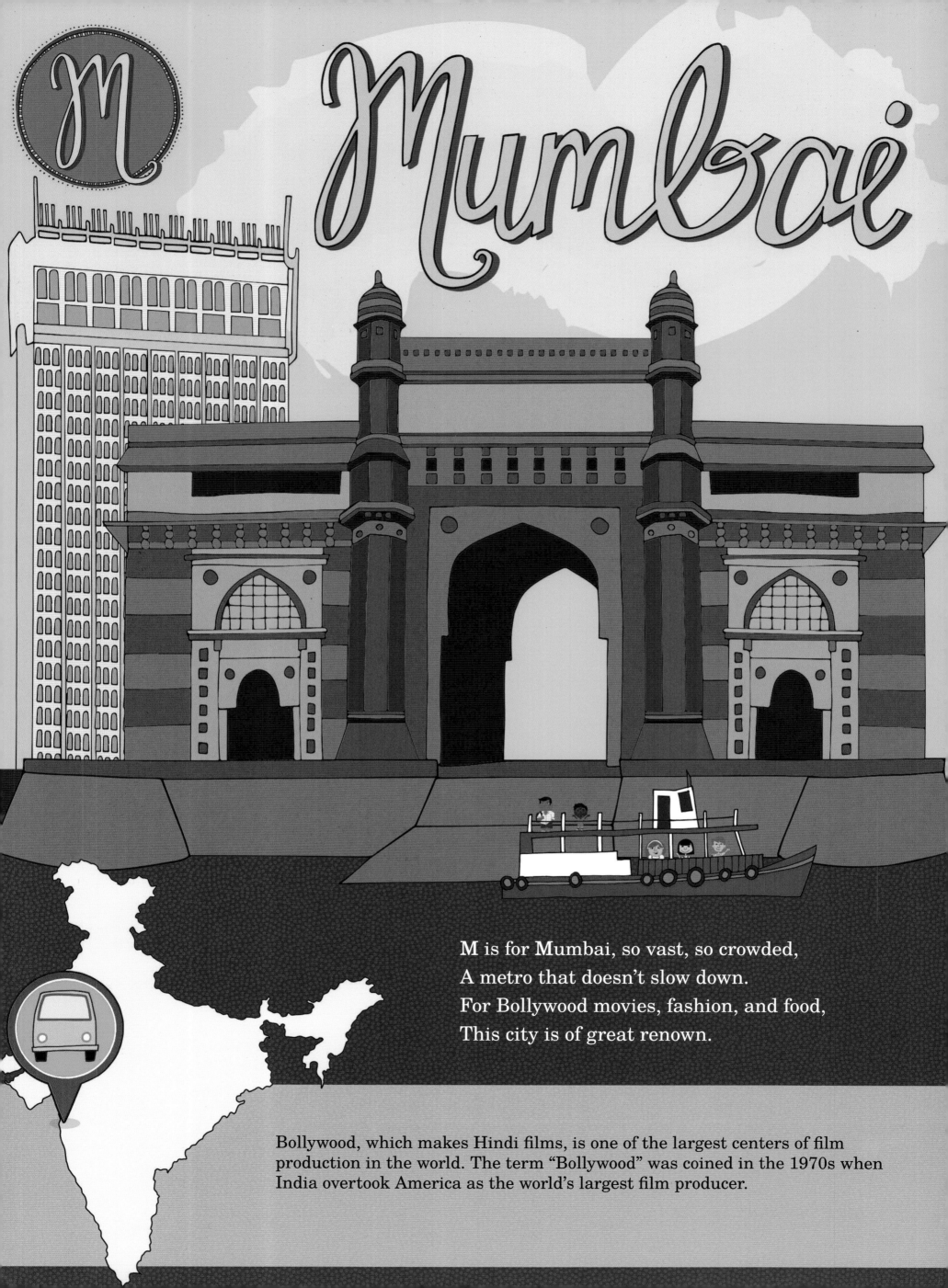

M is for Mumbai, so vast, so crowded,
A metro that doesn't slow down.
For Bollywood movies, fashion, and food,
This city is of great renown.

Bollywood, which makes Hindi films, is one of the largest centers of film production in the world. The term "Bollywood" was coined in the 1970s when India overtook America as the world's largest film producer.

NAGPUR

N takes us to Nagpur,
Where orange trees abound.
But wild orange tigers
Are not so easily found!

Nagpur is known as the Orange City because of the abundance of these fruit trees in the city. It is also the tiger capital of India as there are many wildlife reserves in the area.

O Ongole

O transports us to warm Ongole
Where the Andhra cattle come from.
Their milk is sweet, their bulls are strong,
And their hide is taut as a drum.

Ongole is known for its Ongole cattle, a breed of oxen. This is one of the major Zebu cattle breeds in the world, and the cattle have humps on their backs.

PURi

P puts us in famed Puri,
With the longest golden beach.
The Konarak temple beckons
And historians come to teach.

Puri is the site of the famous annual chariot festival, "Rath Yatra." Each year new wood chariots are constructed for the festival, but each time they are made in the same size and colour as the year before!

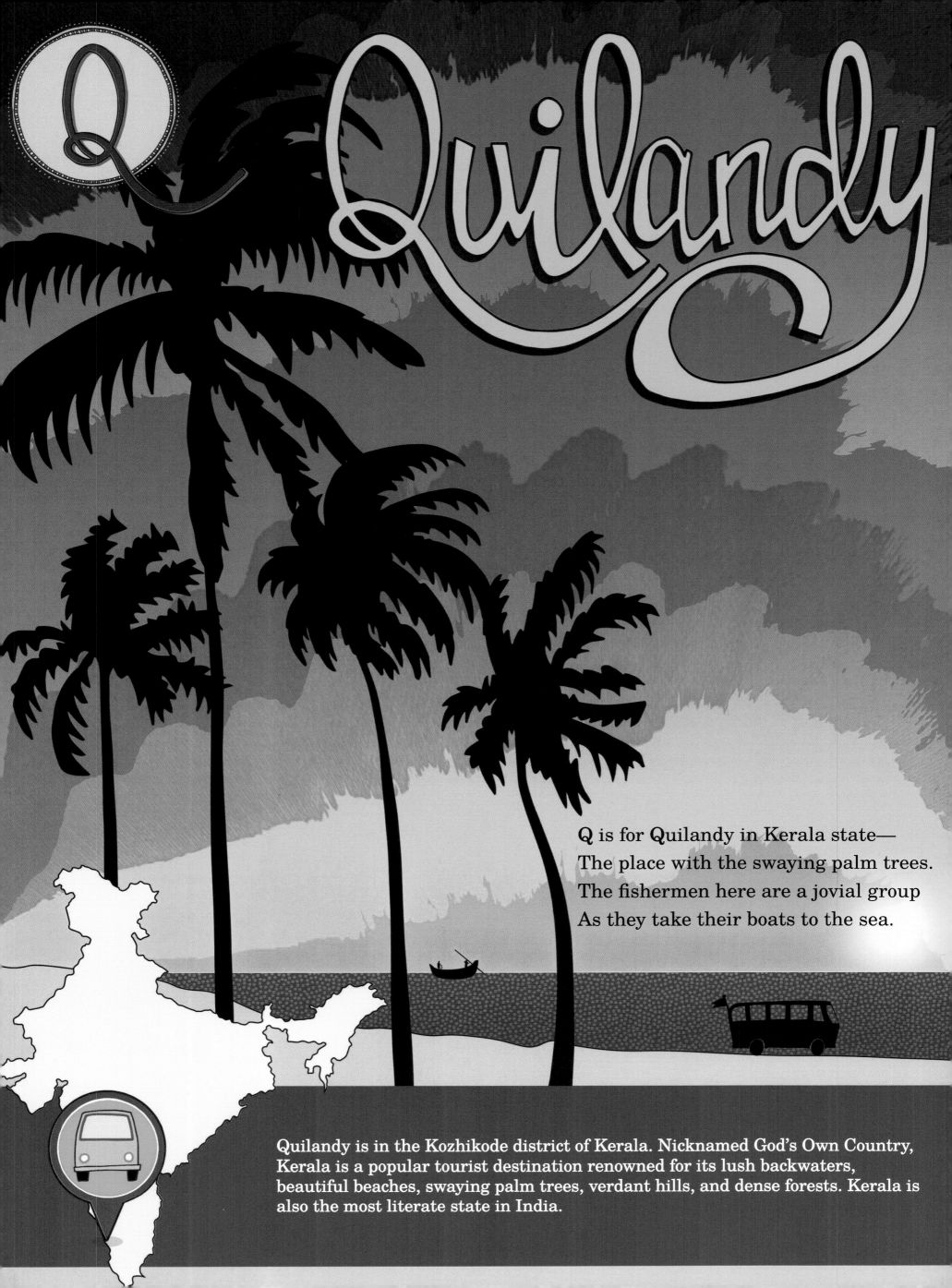

Quilandy

Q is for Quilandy in Kerala state—
The place with the swaying palm trees.
The fishermen here are a jovial group
As they take their boats to the sea.

Quilandy is in the Kozhikode district of Kerala. Nicknamed God's Own Country, Kerala is a popular tourist destination renowned for its lush backwaters, beautiful beaches, swaying palm trees, verdant hills, and dense forests. Kerala is also the most literate state in India.

Rajkot

R for Rajkot, a place of cyclones
That blow and bluster every year.
Gujarat's monsoon rain and storms
Will wash dusty pavements clear.

Rajkot is known for its delicious street food. Vendors for Pav bhaji, chevdo, pani puri, ghugra, vada pav, and samosa dot the streets around the city.

Srinagar

Srinagar in Kashmir is famous for its Pashmina Shawl,
which is popular all over the world today.

S takes us to Srinagar,
Scenic gardens, lakes, houseboats.
Stop to enjoy this magical place
And see graceful shikaras afloat.

The picturesque city of Srinagar is famous for its gardens, waterfronts,
and houseboats. It is also known for traditional Kashmiri handicrafts
and dried fruits.

TURA

T is for Tura in Meghalaya,
The Eastern state of great mystique.
Our bus has come to the Abode of Clouds,
The valley below a high peak.

The British could not pronounce Durama, which was the name for the native god in this place, so they named the town Tura. There are many waterfalls and streams in Tura.

U is for Ujjain, city of temples,
A sacred spot to visit.
In this place where the Lord Krishna studied,
Tourists pour in every minute.

Ujjain is among the "sapta puri" or seven sacred cities in India and is therefore a pilgrimage spot. These cities include Ayodhya, Mathura, Haridwar, Varanasi, Kanchipuram, Dwarka, and Ujjain.

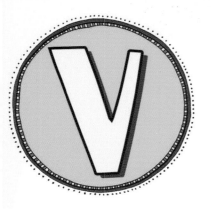

VISAKHAPATNAM

V for Vishakapatnam or Vizag,
The British called it so.
In this old city of seaports and steel,
The rusty shipyard glows.

Vishakapatnam is a large port city on the coast of the Bay of Bengal. It is often called the Jewel of the East Coast.

Warangal

W takes us to Warangal's fort,
And the city's massive stone gateways.
Telugu is spoken in this town,
Where Mughal Aurangzeb used to stay.

This city's residents are called Warangalites. Every year Warangalites celebrate a festival of flowers by taking a different variety of flowers to the temple each day for nine days.

X sounds like exit, but let's keep going!
Our journey still has its allure.
This country is vast, its geography great,
We have two more letters to tour!

Did you know that India is about one-third the size of the US but has more than four times the population?

YANAM

Y is for Yanam, once a French city,
A small district on the Bengal Bay.
People here used to speak the French tongue,
But it's mostly Telugu today.

Yanam was a French colony for 300 years. It was only transferred to
India as a Union Territory in 1954, and some of the older citizens of the
town still speak French.

Zirakpur

Z brings us to Zirakpur,
Where we make our final stop.
We've seen buildings and temples,
Sandy beaches and rivers,
And I'm just about to drop!

Zirakpur is a suburb of Chandigar in Punjab. It is known as the wedding capital of the region as 80% of the wedding banquets and resorts of the Chandigarh tri-city are located in Zirakpur. Wedding fireworks are routinely seen in the town.

Pronunciation Guide

Hi friends, you might notice that our pronunciation guide is a little different from other guides. We use familiar words to make pronunciations easier and more accessible. We hope this helps you learn more about the amazing cultures, religions, and people from India.

Ahmedabad - Eh-m-dha-baadh

Andhra - On-dh-a-raa

Ashram - Aa-sh-rum

Aurangzeb - Or-en-ga-zab

Ayodhya - A-yoo-dh-yaa

Bengali - Ben-gaa-lee

Benguluru - Ben-gaa-loo-roo

Bihar - Bee-haa-r

Braj Bhasha - Braa-j Bhaa-shaa

Chambal - Chaa-m-ball

Charminar - Chaar-mi-naar

Chennai - Chen-eye

Chevdo - Chee-v-dho

Darwaza - Dh-ur-waa-zaa

Durama - Do-raa-maa

Dwaraka - Dh-waa-raa-kaa

Etawah - Ay-thaa-waa

Faridabad - Faa-ree-dha-baadh

Gautama Buddha - Gao-tha-maa Bu-dh-aa

Gaya - Guy-aa

Ghugra - Ghoo-gr-aa

Gujarat - Goo-jaa-raa-th

Haridwar - Haa-ree-dh-waar

Haryana - Haa-ri-yaa-naa

Hindi - Hin-dh-ee

Hooghly - Who-gh-lee

Howrah - How-raah

Hyderabad - Hi-dher-aa-bhaad

Indore - In-door

Jaipur - Jye-poor

Jama Masjid - Jaa-maa Mus-jidh

Jantar Mantar - Jun-th-aar Man-th-aar

Kanchipuram - Caan-jee-poo-rum

Kashmir - Kh-ush-meer

Kerala - Care-uh-laa

Kolkata - Kol-cut-aa

Konark - Koo-naa-rk

Kozhikode - Kho-yee-koh-duh

Krishna - Kri-sh-naa

Pronunciation Guide

Lucknow - Luck-now

Madhya Pradesh - Ma-dh yaa Praa-dh-e-sh

Madras - Maa-dh-raas

Mahatma - Maa-haa-th-maa

Marajaha - Maa-haa-raa-jaa

Mathura - Maa-thoor-aa

Meghalaya - Me-ghaa-la-yaa

Mohandas Karamchand Gandhi - Moe-han-dh-us Kaa-rum-ch-und Gaa-n-dh-ee

Mughal - Mo-gh-al

Mumbai - Mo-m-bay

Nagpur - Naa-g-pur

Nawab - Nah-waa-bh

New Delhi - New Del-he

Ongole - On-go-luh

Pani puri - Paa-nee pur-ee

Patna - Putt-naa

Puri - Poo-ree

Quilandy - Kye-laan-dee

Rajkot - Raaj-kho-t

Rama - Raa-maa

Ramayana - Raa-maa-yaa-naa

Rath Yatra - Raa-th Yaa-th-raa

Rumi - Roo-me

Sabarmati - Saa- baar-muh-thi

Samosa - Saa-mo-saa

Sapta puri - Sup-th-aa poo-ree

Sepoy - Sep-oie

Shikaras - Shee-kaa-ras

Siddhartha - Sid-har-thaa

Srinagar - Sree-naa-gar

Tamil Nadu - Tha-mil Naa-duh

Telugu - Teh-lah-goo

Tura - Thoor-aa

Ujjain - Oo-jay-n

Uttar Pradesh - Oo-th-aar Praa-dh-e-sh

Vada pav - Vaa-daa Paa-v

Varanasi - Vaa-raa-naa-see

Visakhapatnam - Vi-shock-aa-put-nam

Warangal - War-un-gaal

Yamuna - Yaa-moo-naa

Yanam - Yaa-num

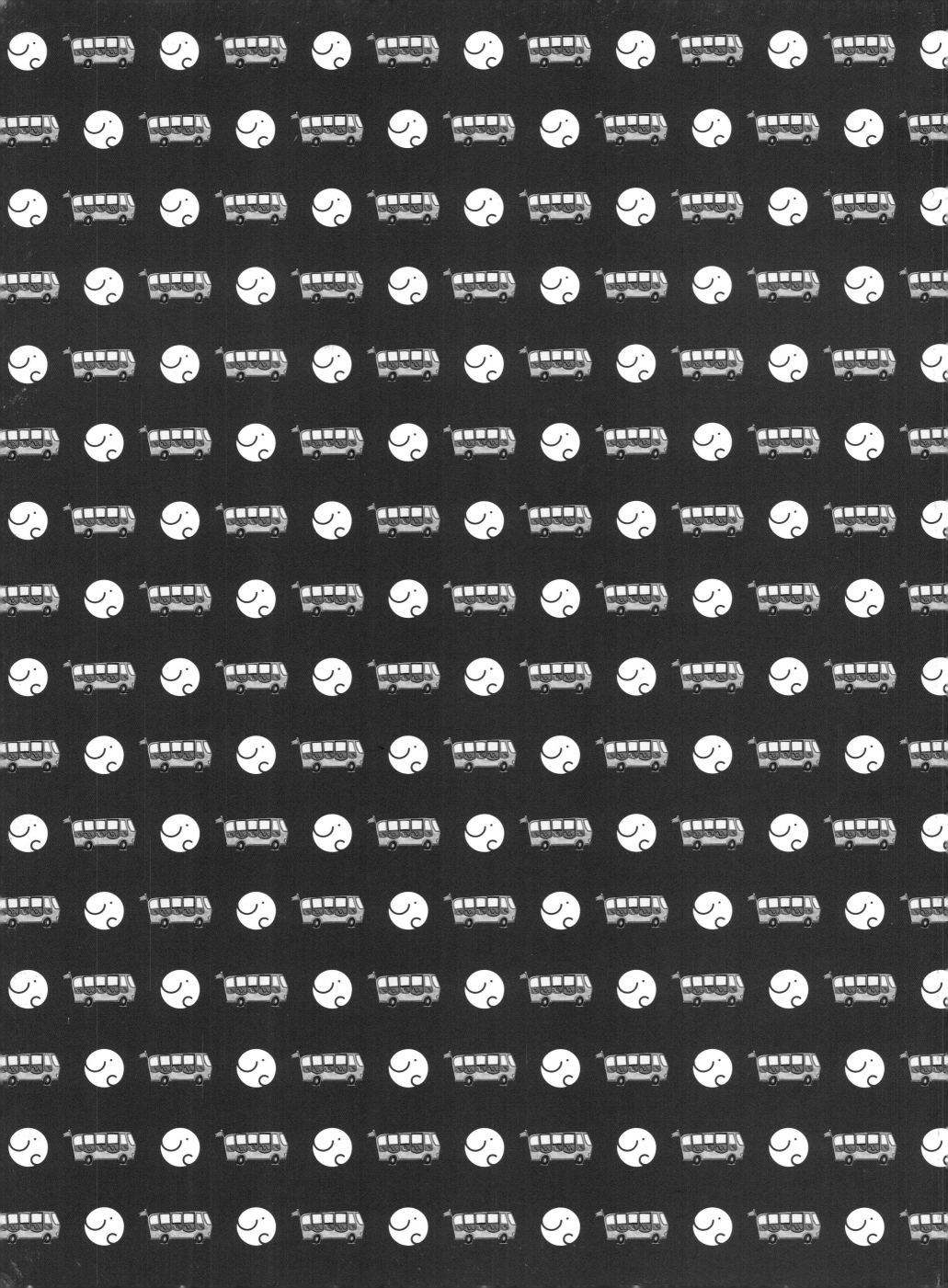